A CHRISTMAS PENGUIN'S WISH

Lenny M. Hill

Merry Christmas
2024!
LmcDermott

 FriesenPress

Suite 300 - 990 Fort St
Victoria, BC, V8V 3K2
Canada

www.friesenpress.com

ISBN
978-1-5255-6829-9 (Hardcover)
978-1-5255-6830-5 (Paperback)
978-1-5255-6831-2 (eBook)

1. JUVENILE FICTION, HOLIDAYS & CELEBRATIONS,
CHRISTMAS & ADVENT

Distributed to the trade by The Ingram Book Company

This book in dedicated to my family.

To my wife, Lorna, thank you for the love and
constant support; to my daughters, Lisa and Jessica,
thank you for the inspiration for this story;
and to my grandchildren, Natalie, Aria, George
and Everleigh—every minute of every day,
you are always in my heart.

It was three days before Christmas and the toy shop was buzzing with families looking for that special gift. The stuffed toys did not show it, but they were just as excited as the shoppers running everywhere—all except for one stuffed penguin. He wasn't excited. He wasn't even happy. All he could think of was why he didn't have a name. Would his Christmas wish come true?

The penguin thought to himself, "All the stuffed toys have names. Why don't I have one, too?" There was Ice Cube the polar bear, Wally the walrus, Sam the seal and Margie, that silly moose over there—all of them had names. Why didn't he have one? The only words on his tag were "Christmas penguin."

"What kind of a name is that?" he said to himself.

Just like children all over the world, stuffed toys have Christmas wishes, too. Their wish is to have a name and to be loved by someone. The Christmas penguin was certain that his wish would never come true.

"After all, what child would want a stuffed toy with no name?" he whispered. He was certain that if no one wanted him, his wish would never come true.

There he sat, on the shelf, waiting for someone to pick him up and make his Christmas wish come true. As the day went on, no one even looked at him.

But then, a little girl walked up to the shelf. She raised her hand towards the penguin, picking him up and turning him around and around. She began to giggle.

"What's so funny?" asked her mom.

"This silly-looking thing doesn't have a name. Why would anyone want it for a present?" said the little girl, dropping the penguin onto the floor. Reaching for the top shelf, she picked up Ice Cube the polar bear instead.

"Mommy, can I have her?" she said. "She is so cool!"

As the little girl turned to run away, her mom quickly hid Ice Cube in her cart.

The next day, a brown-haired boy grabbed Wally the walrus and hugged him, saying "I love you and I want you for Christmas!"

Wally smiled as the boy carried him away, which made the Christmas penguin happy and sad at the same time. He was happy for Wally, but also sad because he himself wasn't leaving the store with a loving child.

It was now Christmas Eve and the store was crawling with last-minute shoppers. The Christmas penguin sat on the shelf looking at all the crazy people running around the toy shop.

Suddenly, a little girl picked up the Christmas penguin and began to turn him over and over.

"This is it, I am going to be her Christmas toy, be loved and have my own name!" he told himself, feeling very good inside.

But there was something wrong, The little girl wasn't smiling.

"What's wrong?" her dad asked.

"Daddy, I don't want this silly penguin. He doesn't have a name, and besides he looks funny!" said the little girl. She tossed the Christmas penguin back on the shelf and ran over to pick up Margie the moose.

It's a good thing that stuffed toys don't cry on the outside, because the Christmas penguin was crying on the inside.

Now the store was closing in five minutes, and everyone seemed to be done shopping. Almost all the shoppers were gone, and the only stuffed toys left in the store were Sam the seal and the Christmas penguin.

Suddenly a man ran into the store. He went straight towards the stuffed toys and grabbed Sam off the shelf, then rushed towards the checkout.

"Can you wrap this up for my son, please?" he begged the teller, who quickly wrapped up Sam and sent the man on his way.

"That's it, we are closed!" shouted Mrs. Brown, the store-owner, as she turned out the lights and locked the front door. Now the Christmas penguin was alone in the cold, dark store. His stuffed heart began to beat a little faster. He was alone, cold and not sure what was going to happen next.

As the penguin began to feel sad and lonely, he heard a sound outside the store. He was now sad, lonely and scared. Suddenly he was grabbed by what felt like a fur-covered hand and stuffed into a big dark bag.

The next thing he knew, he was floating through the air along with what appeared to be other toys. From outside the bag he heard, "Now Dasher! Now Dancer!" The rest faded away as the bag began to drop towards to ground. There was a thud as the flying stopped. What was going to happen next?

With a whoosh, the Christmas penguin went from the cozy bag to a spot under a shiny Christmas tree, filled with colourful lights and surrounded by all sorts of brightly wrapped gifts. The Christmas penguin was too tired to think or worry about where he was or what was going to happen next. He closed his eyes and fell into a deep sleep.

As he began to wake up, the Christmas penguin heard people talking and children laughing. He opened his eyes just in time to see a little red-haired girl grab him from under the tree.

"Lisa, do you like what Santa brought you?" asked her mom.

"Oh yes I do!" shouted Lisa.

As the Christmas penguin did not have a name, Lisa tried to think of one for him. Looking at his fuzzy black coat, Lisa said, "You are so hairy!"

His funny smile made Lisa think about a cat she once saw with the same kind of funny smile. The cat's name was Gilbert.

"That's it," said Lisa. "I am going to name you Harry Gilbert. That would be the perfect name for a 'Harry' penguin with a silly smile!"

The Christmas penguin could hardly believe his stuffed ears.

"I love you, Harry Gilbert. I love you so much," Lisa whispered as she hugged the penguin close.

At Christmas, wishes do come true, even for stuffed toys. The Christmas penguin was as happy as any stuffed toy could be. He now had a name and a person to love him.

"Thank you, Santa, thank you so much!" Harry Gilbert whispered. He smiled and felt warm inside, sitting on Lisa's bed and waiting for another hug.

Lenny M. Hill

I am a recently retired teacher, with a Bachelor's Degree in Education. Having taught 32 years in various small communities in the Northwest Territories. I know that children all around the world have dreams and sometimes, if they are lucky enough, these dreams come true. This is a story that I told to my daughters Jessica and Lisa, when Lisa asked about how she got her penguin for Christmas. My daughters have encouraged me for years to write this story. I told them that I would write it if they did the illustrations so here we are. I hope that children, reading this story, continue to dream.

CPSIA information can be obtained
at www.ICGtesting.com
Printed in the USA
BVHW021628021120
592189BV00001B/2

9 781525 568305